# LOVED BY THE MOUNTAIN MAN

## WILD HEART MOUNTAIN: MILITARY HEROES
### BOOK ONE

SADIE KING

# LOVED BY THE MOUNTAIN MAN

## WILD HEART MOUNTAIN: MILITARY HEROES BOOK ONE

**A forced proximity, age gap romance between a damaged ex-military hero and the curvy girl who heals his heart.**

She's too young, too innocent and too damn happy…

But I can't get the quirky, curvy Hailey out of my head. When she's forced to spend a night in my cabin, she'll find out just how damaged I am.

I faced the enemy in Iraq, but it's nothing compared to the raw vulnerability I feel when Hailey holds my heart in her hands. Can she see past the scars, the limp, and the age gap, or was it pity that brought her to my bed?

*Loved by the Mountain Man* is a forced proximity, ex-military, age gap, instalove romance featuring a scarred military mountain man and the curvy, innocent heroine who may be the healing balm this damaged hero needs.

1

KOBE

*D*ark clouds envelop the mountain as I pull into the parking lot of Angie's Bar. My knee twinges as I climb out of my pickup and I rub it absently, trying to get blood into the damaged tissue. If I didn't already know by the clouds, my bad leg is a pretty good barometer of when it's going to snow.

It's not a good night to be out, but I never miss a vets night with the former Marines from my old unit.

If I didn't organize these monthly meet ups, I doubt some of them would come down the mountain at all. The mountains are a good place for hiding and healing, which is why so many of us ended up back here on Wild Heart Mountain.

Some days I'm not sure which one I'm doing.

A blast of warm air greets me as I cross the

threshold of Angie's Bar. She's got the fire blasting even though the place is almost empty. I make a mental note to bring more firewood next time I'm in town. She'll need it if she has the fire going every night.

A couple of the guys are already at a table near the dartboard. I give them a nod before heading to the bar.

Angie gives me a tired smile. "Looks like snow tonight."

I give her a quick peck on the cheek, and when I look up, Corbin's eyeing me with his brows furrowed.

I tilt my hand to my mouth, silently asking if he needs another drink.

He gives me a nod and keeps his eyes on us.

If I didn't know Corbin better, I'd probably be terrified of his intense looks. But quiet and brooding is just his way.

Angie's kids are at a booth in the restaurant area with homework spread out on the table. And aside from our group, there's only one other table of diners.

It's worrying how empty the place is. I grew up with Angie and her husband. He was the only one in our unit who didn't come home.

She struggles with this place, not that she'd ever admit it. Her family opened the bar back in the nineties and named it after her. When we were kids, this was the only bar in town and the center of the community. It got run down over the years, and Angie and Paul were going to bring it back to life.

They did some renovations every time he was back on leave, and his plan was to retire from the military and help her run the place.

Now she's stuck with a half renovated bar and two kids to raise on her own.

Any of us would step up to help out Paul's widow, but she won't accept money from us. So we find other ways to help.

Which is why I brought my tool kit in with me.

"Where's the door that needs fixing?" I ask.

"Upstairs. Damn lock's broken, and I've got a tenant."

My eyebrows raise in surprise. Angie's got a spare room above the bar that she rents out on short lease. It's easy to find tenants during the tourist season, but with winter coming there aren't many travelers to the mountain.

"She's a young girl who's helping me out at the bar for a few weeks. She's not in town for much longer, but I can't have her staying with a door that doesn't lock."

I wonder what kind of crazy kid comes to the mountain in winter. But it's extra income for Angie, so thank God for the crazies.

"I'll say hello to the boys, then I'll head up."

At that moment, one of her kids comes running over. Her hair is wild, there's a hole in her woolen sweater, and her shoes look almost worn. It breaks my heart to see Paul's kids like this. But Angie's too proud to take cash.

"Hey, sweetheart." I bend down so I'm level with the little girl. Fran is five years old and doesn't remember her Daddy. I slide a twenty-dollar bill into her hand.

"Go share this with your brother."

The little girl's face lights up.

"Can I spend it on candy?" She looks up at her mom with hope in her dark eyes.

Angie gives me a grateful look. "Of course you can, sweetheart."

The little girl throws her arms around my neck. "Thank you, Uncle Kobe."

Then she skips off, waving the bill excitedly to show her brother.

I pull myself up, ignoring the protest from my leg.

"You shouldn't have." But Angie's giving me a thankful look.

"You know, I'll be more than happy to help. If you need money for winter clothes or anything…"

It's useless trying to finish. Angie's already

shaking her head. Her damn mountain pride won't let her take a handout.

"Thanks, Kobe. You do enough already. You guys all do. I've had Corbin in all week cutting firewood for me. And he fixed my car, which saves me a trip to the mechanic. I appreciate all that you guys do, really."

It's been over four years since she lost her husband, and I know how hard that was on her, but I never see Angie complain. At least she's got the bar to keep her busy, and the kids are a comfort. Paul was loved by everybody here. No one's gonna let his widow and kids go without.

"Wrap up warm tonight. That snow's gonna get bad."

"I will."

The guys have chosen a table in the darkest corner of the bar, which is no surprise. My former Marine buddies gravitate to the shadows. Even if the dartboard wasn't over here, they'd still find the darkest corner to sit in.

Rhys was the one that got us all into darts while we were on tour. He got a board from somewhere, and we set it up in the mess. Then he'd thrash us night after night, hitting straight bullseyes.

He was good, could have gone professional if

he'd wanted to. He tells us it was from a misspent youth.

Rhys is focused on the dartboard. His hands are trembling, but we all ignore it, since that's what he's doing.

That's what life is when you return from war. You have to learn to live with the things you brought back with you. Reframe your life to incorporate the damages.

To reiterate my thoughts, my leg gives a twinge, and I grit my teeth. I've gotten used to walking with a limp, but I don't like anyone seeing how much it pains me.

Rhys takes the shot and it hits just off the bullseye.

"Nice shot, man," Corbin says.

Rhys just grunts and grabs one of the beers I've set on the table.

Sometimes when we were on tour, we'd put bets on how many bullseyes he'd get in a night. I haven't seen him get one since we've been back.

The fact that he's still playing is a testament to the man's tenacity. A lesser man might have given up, but not Rhys. When there's something he wants, he won't stop till he gets it.

Rhys is intense and brooding, just like Corbin. He was the deadliest sniper in our platoon. He could creep up on anyone. The man still scares the bejesus out of me.

He guzzles his beer, and I'm wondering if he's trying to see if alcohol can stop the tremors.

My phone buzzes in my pocket, and it's a message from Dylon, telling me he's not going to make it because his babysitter fell through.

Dylon must have been through every willing babysitter on the mountain. But he's a grumpy son of a bitch, and there aren't many babysitters willing to trek that far into the mountain to his remote cabin.

Dylon left the military when his wife passed, and he's never forgiven himself for not being there for her. I was hoping he would be here tonight. Social contact is good for these guys, but I have to practically pull them out of their cabins sometimes. Like I said, it's a great place to heal, and a great place to hide.

The door busts open and Symon strides through, stomping his boots on the mat and clapping his hands together.

"Snow's started."

His voice booms across the room, causing the table of diners to pause in their meals and look up. Symon gives them a friendly nod and a wave.

As a volunteer Ranger, he's gotten to know quite

a few people around the town and is the only one of us that doesn't seem to mind human interaction.

"Sorry I'm late, guys." He slides into a chair next to me, and I hand him a beer.

"A couple of tourists got lost," Symon continues. "With the snowstorm coming it was all hands on deck to find them." Symon shakes his head in mock disgust. "Damn tourists. Who goes hiking when there's a storm coming?"

"Who comes out to a bar when there's a storm coming?" quips Corbin.

"Touché." Symon holds his beer up, and we all knock bottles. "I didn't want to miss your ugly mugs."

Symon's the joker of the group, and lord knows we all need that.

He launches into an account of his afternoon tracking down tourists, gesticulating wildly and making even Corbin crack a smile, almost.

The windowpane rattles, drawing my attention to how the wind's picked up.

"Hate to say it fellas, but we should probably eat and go."

Corbin pushes his chair away and stands up. "I'll ask Angie to get the pizzas on."

We always come to Angie's, and we always order more food than we need and take the leftovers home in doggie bags. It's another little way we can help support her.

While we're waiting for the food, I head upstairs to fix the door. With the storm coming in, I'll want to get away as soon as we've eaten. Not ideal, but when you live on a mountain you learn to respect the weather.

There's no hiding the pain in my leg as I drag it up the metal stairs outside that are already covered in a thin layer of snow. It's slow going with my toolbox in one hand, and I'm glad none of the guys can see how slow I've become. How much less of a man I am than the one that led our unit in Iraq.

As I make my way up the steps, I realize I never asked the name of Angie's tenant.

2
## HAILEY

*H*ot water gushes over me as I rinse the conditioner out of my hair. I give my hips a little shake as I belt out the chorus to Sweet Home Alabama. There's something about being on the road that's got me singing all the big American hits.

I haven't even been to Alabama. Yet. It's on my hit list.

It's been two months since I left Sanborne, my small hometown in rural Virginia. I'm working my way down the east coast states and around the bottom of the Appalachian Mountains to see what's on the other side. Coming from Virginia, I've spent some time in the mountains before. But my travels of the last few months have really opened me up to their beauty. I can see why people come to the mountains of North Carolina, especially Wild Heart Mountain. It's absolutely breathtaking.

I quickly rinse the last of the conditioner out of my hair and turn the shower off. Angie has been a great landlord for these last two weeks, and I don't want to use more hot water than necessary. Any single mom running a business and raising two kids on their own needs all the help they can get. I've been working the bar for her and helping out with odd jobs, but she's given me tonight off and I don't intend to waste it.

I'm washing my hair, I'm going to put on a face mask, make myself cheesy pasta, and veg out in front of the TV. It's a small box TV and there's no cable, but I found a channel that's playing The Bachelor at 9 o'clock. I've got a date. Me, the TV, and cheesy pasta.

I feel a pang of sadness that Trish isn't here to watch it with me. I always watch The Bachelor with my sister, but other than that, it's a pretty perfect night.

I read somewhere that two weeks is the optimal time to stay in a transitory job, so that's how long I told Angie I was staying for. She was grateful for the help, and I accepted minimum wage because I could see she couldn't afford much else.

I get the room for free and a hot meal every day. It's not much, but it's enough for the bus fare to the next town and a few nights' accommodation if I don't find work immediately. Luckily the entertainment is free around here. On my days off, I've been wandering the trails in the mountains taking in the wildlife and the beauty.

It's low tourist season, but plenty of places need help redecorating or deep cleaning in the off season.

I'm happy to turn my hand to anything. On the road I've tried cleaning, painting, nannying, bar work, mending fences, turning soil, and looking after pigs. The smell got to me on that last one.

But I still haven't found my purpose in life, which is what this whole trip is about.

My sister Trish and all my friends were happy to stay in Sanborne and have babies, but I'm sure there's more to life than that. I just don't know what yet.

Mom never exactly talked to us about a career, and going to college wasn't something anyone in our family does. I'm not sure I want to go and study for years anyway, even if I knew what I wanted to do. I'm hoping by travelling around I'll find my calling, my purpose in life. And it definitely won't be having babies and hooking up with a small-town man who expects me to cook and clean for him for the rest of his life.

No way. I want more out of life than that.

I'm singing at the top of my lungs as my towel

shimmies over my wide ass when I hear a noise in the apartment. It might be Angie bringing up a pizza for dinner. She's good like that. I don't know if it's because she feels like she has to mother me, but I am definitely leaning into that.

I wrap the towel around me and pull open the bathroom door just as there's a loud crash.

My apartment door is wide open, and there's a man standing there. He's silhouetted against the single streetlight from the parking lot below. He looks as big as the mountain, and he's carrying an axe.

I scream.

This is what my sister warned me about when I told her I was going travelling. She warned me I'd get murdered in some small town.

The man is so big he takes up the whole door frame, his broad shoulders barely fitting in the door-way. His coat hangs open, giving me a peek of a tight T-shirt and a hint of muscles, which is weird. I didn't expect an axe murderer to be wielding such defined pecs. You never see that in the horror movies.

The man takes a step towards me, and I scream again. There's a snow globe of the mountain sitting on the dresser, and I pick it up and launch it at him.

Unfortunately, sport has never been my strong suit.

The snow globe goes so wide he doesn't even duck. It misses the man completely and smashes through the window beside the door. The tinkling sound of breaking glass fills the silence.

"I suppose I'm gonna have to fix that window too."

His voice is as low and rumbly as the dark clouds rolling in off the mountain and sends my nipples into hard peaks.

Axe murderers are never this sexy in the films.

But instead of moving toward me, the man-mountain slowly drops the axe. Now that I look at it properly, it's not an axe. It's a bright yellow toolbox.

He raises his hands in a placating gesture. Big hands. Rough hands. Working man's hands with calluses. The thought of those rough hands running over my skin and snagging on my nipples fills my brain so utterly that for a moment I can only gape at them.

"You're Angie's tenant, right?"

There's that voice again, low and rumbling, sending tremors through my body and causing my own personal earthquake.

He knows Angie, and I'm beginning to think he's not here to murder me.

His eyes flick down my body. My body that's only covered in a towel.

It's a big body. I'm not complaining, but the

towels here are threadbare and barely bigger than a dishcloth.

I pull the towel tighter around me, unsuccessfully attempting to cover all of my curves.

Yes," I squeak.

"I'm Kobe," the mountain man says. "Angie sent me to fix your door. And I guess you want that window fixed too?"

My racing heart starts to calm. He's not here to ravish me and murder me. A little part of me feels disappointed. Not at the murdering part, but a ravishing by this man? That's something I could get behind, or under as the case may be.

As realization sets in that I've just thrown a snow globe at a very sexy man who's come to do some building maintenance, my cheeks flush.

"Umm. Yeah. The lock's broken," I say with as much dignity as a large girl in a towel the size of a postage stamp can muster. His eyes travel down my body, and I flush under his gaze.

I'm a curvy girl and I love my body, but I can't help wondering what this man thinks of me. By the time he's taking to look me over, I have a suspicion he's quite partial to curvy girls. Or maybe there aren't many women on the mountain, and he is still thinking of ravishing me. My nipples perk up hopefully at the thought.

"Mind if I get to work?"

I realize I'm still staring at him, and heat rises to my cheeks.

"Sure," I squeak. "I'm just gonna get changed."

It's a studio apartment, and the bed takes up one wall. My open bag lies on the floor between the bed and the door, right next to Kobe.

His gaze follows mine, and the heat intensifies in my cheeks. My underwear is strewn on top of my open bag. White cotton panties with a lace trim. I snatch up the panties and quickly grab some other clothes and scurry back into the bathroom, shutting the door firmly behind me. I lean on the back of the door, needing to breathe.

I don't know if it's the heating on full bore or the sexy definitely-not-an-axe-murderer man out there, but it's suddenly burning hot in this place.

3

# KOBE

The woman looks terrified. I don't blame her; I know how I must look with my large physique, the scar across my cheek, and the thick beard that tries to hide it. At least she can't see the limp.

I'm a monster, and even more so compared to this pretty young thing.

The towel she's got wrapped around her doesn't quite cover her full curvy body. A thick creamy thigh peeps out from under the towel and her breasts are pushed together, forming a deep crevice of pillowy flesh.

It's been a hell of a long time since I saw a woman that looked this good. I have to force myself not to lick my lips. Seeing flashes of her skin makes me want to pull that towel off and see what's at the top of those thick thighs.

Then she screams. An ear-shattering, fantasy-piercing scream. Reminding me what a monster I am. That there's no way in hell I'd have a chance with this young beauty. I'm damaged goods, and she's a fucking fairytale princess.

I should be trying to calm her fears, but I'm frozen to the spot. Dumbstruck by her beauty, her long wet hair and pure blue eyes.

She picks something up from the dresser and launches it at me. I'm too stunned to move, but the shot goes wide anyway. The object flies right through the curtain and smashes the window. One more thing I'll have to fix for Angie.

"I suppose I'm gonna have to fix that window too?"

The woman's still gaping at me. It's clear she thinks I'm here to hurt her. I put the toolbox down and raise my hands, showing her I mean her no harm.

"You're Angie's tenant, right?"

She gives a small nod, and the terror starts to go out of her eyes.

It's like she suddenly becomes aware of where she is and the fact that she's in the world's tiniest towel. She shrugs it around her chest and it rides further up her thighs. I try not to look. I really, really try not to look, but Goddamn those thick thighs are too juicy. I want to bury my head between them until this woman screams my name.

I shake the thought out of my head, but my cock takes longer to get the message. I'm rock hard, and the only reason she doesn't notice is because my coat is zipped at the bottom, hiding my painful erection.

It doesn't help that her bag is open and white cotton panties with delicate lace trim are on top. Imagining her in those panties almost has me sinking to my knees in front of her.

Finally, I get through to the woman that I'm here to fix the door, not to murder her, because it's pretty clear that's what she was thinking.

While I get to work, she scurries into the bathroom and gets herself dressed.

It doesn't take long to put a new lock on the door. The window will take longer to fix. I'm gonna have to call in a favor from a buddy to get the glass replaced, and that's not gonna happen overnight.

There's a stack of newspaper on the landing, and I tape up the window, then wrap up the broken glass. It'll hold for a few days until I can arrange to have it fixed.

By the time I'm done, the woman is back in the room sitting nervously on the edge of the bed. She's dressed in leggings and a casual sweater that clings to her body, giving shape to the perfect breasts that I almost got a peek of.

"I'm Kobe. A friend of Angie's."

"I'm Hailey." The woman holds up her hand. "Sorry, I thought you were here to…"

She trails off, embarrassed.

"Murder you?" I suggest.

She bites the bottom lip.

"Sorry. You're just so…?"

Hideous? Monstrous? Terrifying?

"…big," she finishes.

Hailey's curvy and petite. I could scoop her up, throw her over my shoulder, and hike up the mountain with her without breaking a sweat. Or I could have before I injured my leg.

She's brushing out her wet hair. It's dark and ashy colored, but I bet when it dries it'll be silky blonde. I really want to stick around and see what that looks like.

"You can't stay here tonight."

She frowns. "Why not?"

"There's a storm coming in. It's gonna be freezing with this broken window."

She winces. "Sorry, I can pay for it."

"Don't worry about it. I've got a buddy who's a glazier. And we all work for Angie for free."

She cocks her head like she wants to ask why, but she doesn't.

"I don't have anywhere else to go. I have to stay here."

I rub my beard as if I'm thinking, but I already know what I want to say. Is it deviant? Maybe. Are there expectations? No. But do I want to get to know this woman better? Hell yes.

"You're coming with me."

Her head jerks back, and she looks at me like I'm crazy.

"What do you mean?"

"You can't stay here with that storm coming. I've got a spare room. You'll stay with me."

Something flickers in her eyes that I want to believe is excitement, and then they narrow at me.

"How do I know you're not a murderer? It would be stupid to go stay at a strange man's house."

She's got a point. A very good point. I wouldn't advise any young woman to do what I'm proposing, yet I know we won't be strangers for long. I want to know everything about this woman.

I scratch the side of my face where my scar is. Hailey's eyes flick to it, and I drop my hand quickly. The last thing I want to do is draw attention to my flaws.

"Come down and ask Angie about me. If you feel safe, then come with me. If you don't, then I'll help you find a bed for the night."

Hailey's looking at me thoughtfully, making a decision. Luckily, it's the right one.

"Ok. I'll grab my things."

She stuffs items into her duffel bag, not noticing the relief that washes over me.

I let her go down the stairs first. Mainly because I want to watch her ass, but also because I don't want her to see my limp. I'm not ready to show her that yet; she might change her mind about staying.

4

# HAILEY

I might be crazy.

No, I know I'm crazy, because only a crazy person agrees to go to a strange man's house that's halfway up a mountain during a snowstorm. And not just any strange man; a huge, broad-shouldered, taller than most mountain man who's built so big he looks like he's part of the mountain himself.

Kobe could crush me if he wanted to. I would be powerless if he were to force himself on me.

A delicious shiver goes through my body at the thought, and now I know for sure that I'm crazy.

It's an adventure, I tell myself. And the whole point of leaving home and taking this crazy-ass journey was to have an adventure. It might be foolish, yes, but my skin is tingling all over with excitement. Follow the adventure is my motto for the road, and going up the mountain with a hot mountain man is about the biggest adventure you can have.

Besides, Angie couldn't stop singing Kobe's praises. She said I was in safe hands and he was a proper gentleman. Which is kind of disappointing. I think I'd quite like him not to be a gentleman.

So here we are, with my bag hastily packed and Kobe gallantly carrying it to his pickup truck.

I swing my arms against the cold. I haven't had a chance to pick up a winter coat yet. I thought I'd have more time before the weather closed in, but Mr. Mountain Man predicts a storm.

He throws my bag into the backseat and pulls open my door. But before I can get in, he stops me with his hand on my shoulder.

I turn around casually as if his touch hasn't just set off a hundred nerve endings singing through my body.

"Put this on."

He slides out of his coat and hands it to me. He's only got a long sleeve T-shirt on underneath that clings to him, showing off every delicious muscular curve.

I noticed a slight limp as we walked over to his truck, which has piqued my curiosity. I want to know how he got the scar on his cheek, why he walks with a limp, and how those defined abs feel when I run my fingers over them.

"Won't you be cold?" I draw my gaze away from his abs and up to his chiseled face.

"I'm used to it."

Gratefully, I shrug on his coat and slide into his truck.

We leave the small town behind and head up a winding mountain road. Mountain man knows what he's talking about when it comes to weather, because the snow gets heavier as soon as we set off.

"You live alone?"

I cringe as soon as I've said it. It sounds like I'm fishing for information rather than making conversation. Although I can't help holding my breath waiting for his answer.

"Yup. Just me and the mountain."

He's not got a wife. I don't know why that makes me so happy. I've just met the guy. His fingers drum the steering wheel, and I can't keep my gaze off those hands, so big and rough. I wonder what he does with them all day.

"Do you work up here?"

"Yup."

He's a bit of a one word kind of guy, so I'm surprised when he starts talking in more than one sentence answers. Kobe tells me about his carpentry business, making furniture in the mountains and coming down to help with repairs and maintenance in the town.

I like to hear him talk. His soft, rumbly voice is soothing and comforting. The snow falls silently around us, and my eyelids start to feel heavy.

I don't know how long I doze for, but I'm startled awake by the crunch of gravel as we turn into a driveway.

"You awake, Sleeping Beauty?"

Ohh, I like the way that sounds on his lips.

"Sorry." I turn away discreetly, wiping my mouth in case I was dribbling, which would be totes embarrassing.

Snow is falling heavily now, and the windshield wipers are on full bore. I can just make out a wooden cabin peeking out from between the snow-laden fir trees, its slanted roof heavy with pure white snow.

The snow is thick on the ground but his truck plows through it easily, coming to a stop in front of the cabin. The pieces all slot perfectly together and a string of fairy lights illuminates the porch, with two chairs on the deck facing out to the forest. A warm feeling grows in the pit of my stomach and rises up to fill my chest. It's like déjà vu, as if I've been here before, which is ridiculous because I never have. Or maybe it's the opposite of déjà vu. Maybe I know that this is where I will return to many times.

"It's beautiful."

I step out of the truck, and with the snow falling, I feel like I'm in a Christmas movie. Kobe grabs my bag, and I follow him into the cabin.

The inside is even more impressive than the outside.

It's an open plan kitchen and living area. The back wall is exposed wooden logs, and the front is floor to ceiling windows looking out into the dark forest.

"Wow," is all I can say, because I am utterly speechless. I've never been anywhere this nice before or anywhere that feels so much like home.

"It's even more beautiful in the daylight."

I didn't know Kobe had come up behind me, and his voice makes me jump. He's so close his breath tickles the back of my neck, making the tiny hairs stand up on end.

"You can see right down to the valley."

"Wow."

I seem to be at a loss for words, because I'm repeating myself here. In all my travels, I've never seen anything so beautiful.

"I'll get the fire going, and then I'll get us something to eat. Any requests?"

A fire and a hot meal and a proper log cabin with a mountain man. This is one adventure I'm not going to forget.

5

KOBE

Two hours later, I've got the fire blazing, and we're sitting in front of the TV watching The fucking Bachelor. Well, Hailey's watching The Bachelor, and I'm watching Hailey. I don't care for reality TV, but I'll watch it every damn day of the week if it means hanging out with Hailey.

She's sitting on the couch and I'm on the chair, which I've positioned slightly back from her so she can't see that I can't take my eyes off of her.

Her hair is dry now, and it's a dusty blonde that falls in waves down her shoulders. Just before dinner, she scooped it up and tied it in a messy knot, and escaped tendrils are teasing the back of her neck. I long to sweep them out of the way and plant my lips there.

Hailey tilts her head back and laughs at something on the screen. I made dinner earlier, cheesy pasta at her request, and a bit of gloopy cheese clings to the corner of her mouth. As she laughs, it stretches from one lip to the other. It should be gross, but it's endearing. I'm jealous of that cheese.

I have to sit on my hands to keep from reaching out and touching her. Jesus, what is wrong with me? I've been a happy bachelor for thirty-nine years, and now here I am going gaga over a woman just because she's got soft-looking hair and cheese on her lips.

*But she's not just any woman,* my heart whispers. *She's* your *woman.*

One of the characters on screen gets emotional and Hailey leans forward, absorbed in the drama playing out.

I take the opportunity to scoop up the plates and take them to the kitchen. I'm not interested in The Bachelor. But I sure as hell am interested in Hailey. I've been waiting for this damn show to finish so I can find out more about her.

I finish up the dishes and make cups of hot cocoa for the both of us. The Bachelor's just finishing up when I bring them through to the lounge.

This time I take a seat on the sofa next to her as I hand her a steaming mug.

Hailey's already told me a little bit about her background, where she grew up and the sister she left behind. But I want to know more.

"How long have you been on the road?"

She blows on her cocoa to cool it down, her lips pouting together in a way that makes my dick pay attention. I shift on the couch so she can't see my growing hard-on.

"I left about two months ago."

"Why? What makes a young woman go off on her own?"

I love that she's got an adventurous spirit, but I'm curious and fearful for her. It can't be safe travelling alone.

Hailey shrugs. "I come from a small town. And I didn't wanna end up like my sister and like my friends."

"Why? What have they got themselves into?"

My mind's racing, imagining petty crime or some small town drug situation.

"Babies." She says it with her nose wrinkled up, as if the thought of babies is something disgusting to her. "Literally every single one of my friends, and now my sister, are having babies. I've got nothing against babies, but there's got to be more to life, right?"

A pang of disappointment hits me. I've been thinking about Hailey having my babies ever since she walked into my cabin and made it feel like a home for the first time.

"You never want babies?"

She doesn't notice the way I'm hanging on her answer.

"Eventually, but I'm only twenty-two. I'm not ready for that yet."

Relief floods me as she keeps talking.

"My sister is with this guy who grew up on the next street over from us. He doesn't treat her well. I wanted her to come travelling with me. I thought if she got out and saw the world, she might see that there are other men out there who would appreciate her more. But now she's pregnant, so…"

Hailey shakes her head, and there's sadness in her eyes as if her sister being pregnant is the worst thing in the world.

"Isn't it something to celebrate?"

"You'd think so. I just wish her boyfriend wasn't such a douchebag."

She's obviously anxious about her sister, and I hate seeing the worry that creases her forehead.

"You want something better for her?"

"I want something better for all of them."

She must see my confusion.

"I mean the girls back home. It's like that was what was expected of us, to get knocked up young and have babies. I just wanted to get out and see the world."

"That's fair enough." I remember that same feeling when I joined the military. I hated growing up in a small mountain town. "Joining the Marines felt the same way. I wanted an adventure."

Her voice goes quiet.

"How long did you serve?"

I hate talking about the military. It drags up a lot of stuff for me, not all of it good. Instinctually, my hand goes to my scar, and I pull it away before I can touch it.

"Too long," I tell her. "I made the spare room up for you."

She looks at me for a long time but doesn't challenge the subject change.

"Thank you. I appreciate it."

As we've been talking, Hailey put her feet up on the couch. Now she slides them along the couch so that her toes wiggle against my leg. I put my hand around her sock clad feet and start massaging.

I can't help myself; I need to touch her.

She looks at me shyly and doesn't pull back, which makes me think she likes it. She sets her cocoa down on the table and scoots up so that she's next to me.

"Thank you for your service."

Her face is close to mine and I take her cheeks in

my hands, feeling her hot breath on my skin. She's stirring up feelings inside of me, desire, need, and longing. A deep longing to have a woman in my life, to have *this* woman in my life. I'm not sure what she sees in a man like me, but she's here letting me touch her with her lips parted in anticipation.

I press my mouth against hers, pulling her into a kiss. She tastes like cocoa and cheese, sweetness and light and all the things I fought for during those long, hard years. All the goodness that I came home for but never found until now, with this woman.

Hailey pulls away from the kiss, and her green eyes are sparkling with emotion. Her hand runs up to my face, and before I can stop it, her fingers trace the line of my scar.

She doesn't say anything. She just leans forward and kisses the puckered skin. I try to hide the scar with my beard, but the bristles grow patchy over the dead skin. It must feel hideous under her gentle lips.

When she pulls back, there are tears in her eyes. And that's when it hits me. This is a pity kiss. Hailey feels sorry for me, and this is what she's doing. To thank me for my service.

I stand up abruptly.

"You don't have to feel sorry for me, Hailey."

There's a wounded look in her eyes, but I walk away. The last thing I need is pity, especially from Sleeping fucking Beauty.

"Your room's down the hall."

I stride out of the room and straight to my bedroom, pulling the door closed behind me and leaving Hailey in the lounge.

I don't know what the hell I was thinking. Why would a beautiful woman like Hailey want a messed up monster like me?

# 6

# HAILEY

What the heck just happened? Kobe stalked away from me, and I have no idea why. I thought there was something between us. I thought this attraction, this ridiculous, crazy, all-consuming attraction that I have for him, was mutual.

I've seen the way he looks at me. The way he was staring at me all through the TV show like he wanted to pounce on me.

How could I have gotten it so wrong?

Embarrassment enflames my cheeks. I stare at the fire, blazing as intense as the feelings I have burning inside of me right now. I'm so mortified that I want to get out of here and walk down the mountain, even though there's a snowstorm happening outside.

I thought kissing Kobe would be an adventure, one my body was eager to go on. I was so sure that he shared my feelings, right up to the moment when he pulled away after I kissed his scar.

Ah. That's it. I touched his scar.

I wanted to kiss away the hurt. I wanted to let him know that whatever scars he has inside and out, I'm here to heal them.

But maybe it only reminded him of how he got them. Maybe he doesn't think he deserves this. But I can tell he's a good man, and good men are worth fighting for.

Gathering up my courage, not knowing if I'm going to be rejected again, I tentatively knock on his door.

"Kobe?"

There's the sound of weight shifting from behind the door, and I get the feeling he's been leaning on it. Then the door opens. He looks tortured. His eyes are troubled and intense.

"Why did you kiss me?"

He grabs my chin and holds it between his thumb and forefinger, demanding an answer. His fingers press into my flesh, shocking me with how rough he's been and at the same time making my nipples harden.

"Why, Hailey? Why did you kiss me?"

All the feelings bubble up inside of me and come spilling out.

"Because I've been wanting to kiss you ever since you broke open my door. Because even though I barely know you, I know there's a connection between us. Because you might be my best adventure yet."

He stares at me for a long moment.

"Is it pity?"

I'm shocked that he would even think that.

"No, Kobe. Of course not. Why would I pity you? You've done something with purpose in your life, something worthwhile. And yeah, you've got scars, and I can't even begin to imagine what you've been through. But no, I don't pity you. I'm grateful for you, but not pitying."

His hold on me relaxes, but only a little. His thumb moves down my chin and caresses my throat, making me swallow hard under his touch.

"I feel the same, Hailey. I've wanted to kiss you ever since I saw you in that ridiculous towel. It's been driving me nuts having you here and not touching you."

I should run a mile; I should get out while my heart is still intact. But I don't. Life is an adventure, and my gut is telling me to see where this one leads.

"Touch me then, Kobe." My voice is breathless

and needy, and I push my chest out so it presses up against him. "Touch me wherever you want."

## 7

## KOBE

Everything Hailey says to me makes my heart melt. Can I really have a chance with a woman like this?

"You're perfect, Sleeping Beauty."

She smiles shyly at the pet name, and I can tell she likes it. My chest pounds with feelings for this woman, and I want to tell her that I'm falling for her, that I think I love her. But then her mouth is on mine, and there's no need for words.

The kiss is like an awakening inside of me. There's an unfamiliar feeling in my chest, and it takes a few moments to identify it as hope. I haven't felt hope since those first few months as a green military recruit, thinking I really could change the world and make it a better place.

Now hope bursts in my chest. Hope that maybe

I'm good enough for a woman like Hailey. That she can see past my scars, past my limp, past my damaged soul. That we could have a future together, a family on my mountain, making the world a better place for those we love.

The kiss deepens, and my passion for this woman overwhelms me.

I push her across the hallway, pushing her up against the wall. She gasps as I press myself against her, grinding my hardness into her soft belly. Now that I've got her in my arms, I'm filled with a need to ravish her, to make her mine.

"You're already hard."

She sounds surprised as she feels me pressed up against her.

"Honey, I've been hard ever since I saw you struggling to keep that poor excuse for a towel around you."

Hailey chuckles, a deep and throaty sound that sends tremors down to my cock. This woman does things to me that I cannot explain.

As I kiss her mouth, her hands run down the back of my spine and over my hips, every brush of her fingers making me crazy. She fumbles for my belt buckle, but if she touches my cock even one little bit, I'm gonna explode right now. And I don't want to explode until I've made her scream my name from that pretty little mouth.

My hands slide to hers, and I wrap them around her wrists. She gasps as I pull them above her head and gives me an annoyed pout.

"Not fair."

"I'm not playing fair."

Her wrists are so small that I can use one of my big, rough hands to pin her against the wall while the other hand slides down her body.

She lets out a moan as my fingers trail down her neck and over her breasts. Her eyes flicker shut.

I like it like this. With her body up against the wall, her tits are pushed out, and I use my spare hand to slide up her T-shirt and grasp her firm, heavy breasts.

One hand unhooks her bra, and then my fingers are running over her soft, soft skin. My rough calluses press into her delicate flesh and catch on her nipples.

She feels so soft and fresh, and I'm reminded that there's a seventeen year age difference between us. I'm a rough, grizzled old man beside this young, innocent, sweet flower.

The thought excites me, and my cock leaks pre-cum in my pants. I want to plant my seed in this flower. I want to mark her and make her mine.

My thumb strums her nipple, making Hailey groan, and it's the sweetest sound I've ever heard. Using my forefinger and thumb I pinch her nipple, rolling it between my fingers. She bucks against me, writhing her body in agonized ecstasy.

"Kobe," she whines. "It's not fair."

Her hands struggle in my grasp, but I'm too strong for her.

"I wanna touch you."

"I'll do the touching, sweetheart." She doesn't realize that if she touched me now, I'd go off like a firework. This woman's got my balls pulled up so tight I'm almost coming just looking at her.

My spare hand travels over her stomach to the top of her leggings. She pushes her hips forward, wanting me to touch her pussy and relieve her friction, but I'm not done playing with her yet.

My hand veers off before I reach her pussy and slides around the back of her leggings and under the elastic. Cupping her buttocks in my hand I squeeze hard, making her gasp.

Her ass is as juicy as the rest of her.

I can't get over how soft her skin feels, how delicate and smooth. My hand slowly slides around to her hip, then to the top of her thigh.

My eyes stay on hers, and I love seeing them widen as my fingers caress the edge of her sticky folds. I feel her need in the dampness, in the whining noise that's coming from her lips, in the pleading look in her eyes. It's like a signal to my cock, which throbs against my jeans screaming to be let out.

I want to fuck this flower; I want to destroy her. But I don't want her to think I'm a monster. So I hold myself back, taking my time caressing her pussy gently while a storm of desire rages inside me.

Reluctantly, I let Hailey's hands go and crouch in front of her before she has time to touch me. My leg smarts, and I swallow down the pain as I shift to my knees. With a quick movement, her leggings are around her ankles and her panties with them.

She gasps as her pussy is exposed to the cold air and gasps again as I pull her leg up. Yanking her leggings and panties off her feet, I toss them aside. She's up against the wall and I part her legs, shifting one of them over my shoulder and opening up her flower. It's my turn to gasp.

From between her pretty pink, glistening lips, a tiny pearl peeps out at me shyly. So sweet, so inviting, so fucking beautiful.

My heart thunders in my chest as I gaze at the beautiful sight before me. This is my future right here, and I'll spend every damn day for the rest of my life on my knees worshiping at this temple.

My thumb runs gently over her delicate pearl.

"Kobe..." Hailey grasps my shoulders, her fingers digging into my flesh.

But it's nothing compared to the reaction when I press my mouth to her flower.

"Kobe!" Hailey screams. And all I've done is

breathe warm air onto her pussy. This woman is a live wire, and she's about to go off.

I press my tongue against her pearl and feel her tremble under me. I want to draw this out for her so I start gently, sucking on her glistening folds and skirting around the pearl, my tongue exploring her pussy as she gets used to the sensations. Only once I feel like my touch won't overwhelm her do I lick her gently, tasting her sweetness and lapping up her juices.

She grabs the back of my head, her fingers tangling in my hair, causing sharp pricks of pain in my scalp, which turns me on even more.

My finger runs around her entrance and when I slide it in, her pussy squeezes me so tight I almost lose sensation in my finger.

This is a woman who hasn't been fucked before. I pull away and look up at Hailey. Her cheeks are flushed pink, and her eyes are dark with desire.

"Are you a virgin, Hailey?"

She's breathing hard, her breath coming in heavy pants. She nods her head.

"Has a man ever touched this?"

My hand slides over virgin pussy, and I clasp her in my hands.

She shakes her head. "No. You're the first, Kobe."

I offer up a silent prayer to the gods, thanking

them for delivering this woman into my life and delivering her untouched.

I'll be her first everything. The weight of that isn't lost on me. I'll make this good for her. I'll give her a first time to remember. I may have come back a broken man, but I can still make a woman scream my name.

I dip my face back to Hailey's pussy, breathing in her musky scent. My tongue laps at her sweet flower, and I push my finger in a little more. With every inch she cries out, grasping my shoulders. I'll have bruises tomorrow, but I'll wear them proudly.

I can't begin to imagine what my cock will feel like in her tight little virgin cunt. But that's not happening yet. First, I'm taking care of her like a man should.

I lick and suck and nip, tasting my girl, loving my girl. Making sure every stroke of my tongue is what she needs. By the way she rubs her face against me, I know I'm giving her everything she needs. Her pussy relaxes and I slide my finger all the way in, but it's not until I slide two inside that she loses control.

Her body convulses, and she screams my name over and over and over like a prayer to the gods.

I keep my mouth on her cunt and my fingers inside her until the orgasm passes. And even then, I don't let up. As soon as the tremors stop, I lick her again.

"Oh no. Oh no," she pants.

I pull my head up. "You want me to stop?"

"No." Hailey shakes her head in frustration. "I don't know if I can handle it, Kobe. It's… the feelings…"

Before I can figure out what's she's trying to say, I've got my head buried between her legs and she's moaning again, her hips pushing into my face.

I glance up and she's leaning back on the wall, her eyes closed, her hands up her shirt playing with her tits.

It's the sexiest thing I've ever seen. I can't wait to get my cock inside this beauty. But not until I've done this properly, until I've proven that I'm not too damaged to satisfy her needs.

I find her hard nub, and this time it only takes a few strokes and a few licks until she's screaming my name and coming again.

I could do this all night. And I do. Every time her orgasm finishes, I bring her to another peak until she's practically sobbing. I know she's had enough when she can no longer keep her leg propped over my shoulder. Only then, as the final orgasm subsides, do I slide her off my shoulder and close her sticky thighs.

My leg screams at me as I drag myself up to a standing position, and I have to look away so she doesn't see the pain. Luckily Hailey's too drowsy to notice.

"That was fucking amazing."

Her words are slurring like she's drunk, and I put my arm around her to stop her from falling over. She leans against me, making my leg scream out. But I don't tell her about my pain.

She doesn't need to know about my sore leg. All she needs to know is that I'm the man who's gonna make her scream his name for the rest of her life. I'm the man who's gonna make her feel good every night for the rest of my fucking life.

I don't tell her that, though. She's too tired, her body a dead weight in my arms.

Feebly she reaches for my belt buckle, but I stop her hand.

"It's all right, honey. Let's get you to bed."

I'll have a sore cock all night, but I can tell she's too tired. I can look after myself later. It was worth it to hear her scream my name over and over again.

"I can't walk," she says, sounding surprised. "I literally can't walk." But she's smiling an amazed smile as she says it, and I love that I've done that to her. Made her come so hard so many times that she can't walk.

We stumble to my room, because there's no way we're sleeping apart tonight. I tuck Hailey under the covers, and before I can even join her, she's breathing deeply, fast asleep.

I take care of myself quickly in the bathroom, thinking about her tight wet cunt. And then I climb into the bed next to her. My arm goes around her body, and I pull her close.

"Good night, Sleeping Beauty," I whisper into her hair.

In the stillness of the night, I can almost believe that she's truly mine.

8

HAILEY

The smell of bacon wafts down the hallway, permeating the blankets, making my nose twitch under the duvet, and pulling me into consciousness.

Trish must be up cooking like she used to before that asshole of a boyfriend appeared on the scene. My bed feels comfier than usual, and I pull the duvet closer and snuggle deeper into the mattress.

Home hasn't felt this cozy for a long time.

But something's different. I can't hear the kids playing in the yard next door or the neighbor's TV that's always blaring. Trish is singing, so at least she's happy, only the rich baritone that's rumbling down the hall isn't Trish's.

My eyes fly open, and I sit up in bed. A luxurious

king size bed with the softest blankets I've ever slept in.

I'm not at home. I'm not in the little two-bedroom apartment I shared with my sister. I'm in a cabin in the middle of the woods, and my very own mountain man is singing in the kitchen.

I slump back on the pillows with a wide grin on my face. This is better than home.

*This is your new home.*

I shake the thought out of my head. I'm here for an adventure, not to fall in love.

*Too late...*

Luckily Kobe walks in at that moment, and I don't have to keep arguing with my inner self. That girl doesn't know when to shut up sometimes.

"You like bacon and eggs?"

He looks even better in the light of day than he did last night, if that's at all possible. Maybe it's because he's carrying a large tray of food, which will always win me over.

My stomach growls and I throw my arms over it, embarrassed. Between dribbling, cheese stuck to my face, and the loudest stomach ever, he must think I'm gross.

Kobe chuckles. "Thought you'd be hungry after last night."

Thoughts of last night flood my brain. Kobe's wicked tongue and the way I wantonly drapped my leg over his shoulder, grinding myself onto his face like a dog in heat.

I put my hands over my eyes and groan, embarrassed that I let myself go so completely.

Kobe slides the tray onto the bed and sits down.

"What are you hiding from, Sleeping Beauty?"

I love the nickname that he's given me, and I peep out at him from between my fingers just in time to see apprehension flicker across his face.

"Do you regret it?"

Do I regret having so many orgasms I couldn't stand straight?

"No."

I smile shyly and Kobe relaxes, making me think I imagined the apprehension.

"Eat."

Kobe slides the tray toward me, and I fall on it hungrily, putting bacon slices between two thick pieces of bread and lavishing it with ketchup.

"Mmm, this is good."

Not only has Kobe given me several orgasms, but last night he made my favorite dinner and today my favorite breakfast. This man is just too perfect.

Foreboding clenches my gut, and I almost choke on my sandwich.

Maybe this is what Trish felt when she met douchebag. Maybe it's easy to woo a woman with food and orgasms, and the next thing you know you're pregnant and stuck with an asshole.

*But Kobe isn't like that.*

The truth is I have no idea what Kobe's like. This thing between us feels real to me, but maybe he does this with every girl that comes to the mountain.

I'm inexperienced with men. All the boys I grew up with threw themselves at any girl they could catch hold of, and I swore I'd never get caught. But I walked right into this mountain man's trap.

"You want coffee with that?"

Kobe smiles at me, and with his wide grin I shake the doubts out of my mind. I'm enjoying this adventure, so why not enjoy it to its end? Whatever that may be.

We finish eating, and he puts the tray on the bedside table and swings his legs over the bed.

What we did last night was all new to me and it felt so amazing, but I don't know how to ask for it again.

"Kobe…"

I bite my bottom lip, unsure of how to go on.

His thumb swipes the corner of my lip.

"You missed some sauce."

He sucks the sauce off his thumb, and I can't take my eyes off his lips. I want to be that thumb. I'm jealous of a thumb. What is this man doing to me?

We move toward each other at the same time,

and our lips collide in the middle. His arms wrap around me, and my hands slide down his muscle-ridged back.

If this is a one-time fling, then I'm going to make the most of it, because I've never felt safer or more taken care of than when I'm with Kobe.

"Kobe…"

I pull away, trying again to ask him for what I want.

My v-card has been hanging over my head for the last few years. I wanted to save it for someone special. And maybe Kobe is special. Or maybe he's just a man who knows how to give a woman what she needs. Either way, I want him to be the one.

"I want you to be my first."

His eyes widen, and flames of desire lash at his irises. His hands cup my cheeks, his callused fingers stroking my soft skin. I close my eyes and lean into his hands. Even this gentle touch does funny things to my body, making electric shocks shoot across my skin and straight down to my lady parts.

He's looking at me so intently that I have to close my eyes before I'm overwhelmed by the emotion that's bubbling up inside me.

"Are you sure, Hailey?"

I nod, and he tilts my head up.

"Open your eyes, sweetheart. I need to hear your words. Tell me what you want."

His voice is husky, and his eyes have gone dark with desire. My own desire grows as I look into those eyes.

"I want you to take my virginity, please."

Kobe sucks in a breath, and a groan escapes his lips.

"That's what you want, sweetheart?"

His hands slide down my throat, making the skin inflamed everywhere he touches. My nipples pebble and wet heat gushes between my legs, drenching my panties.

"Yes, please." My voice comes out as a whisper, making him groan again.

Then his hands are on me, all over my body, pulling my hips toward him and grinding into his hardness. Our mouths collide and we devour each other, the kiss urgent and needy. I can't get enough of him, his taste, his scent, and his hard cock that's pressing into my belly.

We pull at each other's clothes until they're discarded on the floor and our naked bodies are intertwined.

Rough hands rake down my body, and I feel every hard callus as it runs over my skin. His hungry mouth is on my breasts, sucking my nipples while his beard scratches my skin, sending delicious tingles skittering over my body. It happens so fast.

It's overwhelming and wonderful and so full of sensations that I can barely breathe.

His hands slide over my hips and down between the gap between my legs, making me gasp. "You're already wet," Kobe says in wonder, like he doesn't know what he does to me, that his touch has me writhing, needing a release.

His kisses move down my body, landing gently between my legs. One lick from his hungry tongue, and I'm panting already. It's too much, too overwhelming.

"Stop," I pant out, and Kobe backs off. The loss of his mouth on me feels catastrophic.

"No, don't stop."

He raises his eyebrows at me, and I know I'm being contrary, but it's so overwhelming.

"We can stop if you want, sweetheart."

"No. I mean. If you do that again, I'm gonna come. But I wanna feel you inside me this time."

Kobe lets out a long breath between his teeth.

"Okay."

His voice is ragged, like he's trying to contain himself.

That's when I notice his cock. Sticking straight out, the purple veins throbbing and sticky pre-cum dripping from the end.

Wow, just wow.

"It's huge."

I don't know how I'll fit that inside me. Kobe must sense my anxiety, because he takes my hand and wraps it around his thick girth.

"This is all for you, Hailey. And you will take it all. You are made for me. That's why we need to warm you up first."

I get it now.

This time when he ducks between my legs, I don't stop him. Instead, I give in to the sensations of his warm breath, his tongue, his fingers darting in and out of me as his wicked tongue licks my clit until I'm crying out his name, my pussy pulsing.

Only then does he come up for air. His two fingers are glistening with my juices, and he puts them in his mouth and sucks long and hard.

"You taste fucking delicious."

It's so filthy and so erotic.

"Lay back, sweetheart."

He pushes me against the bed and positions himself over the top of me. I'm anxious about what comes next and also excited.

Kobe just made me fall apart, and now I spread my thighs for him, opening myself right up, ready for him to take what he needs from me.

He nestles between my thighs and runs his cock through my sticky pussy folds.

"You ready for me?"

As he says it, the tip of his cock finds my

entrance and rests there, teasing my opening. We're both breathing hard. If he pushes forward, there's no going back. But I don't want him to go back.

"Yeah."

He trembles as his cock slides into me. It's only the tip but it stretches me open, making me gasp at the sensation.

His eyes lock on mine and we pause here, breathing hard until he pushes forward again. It's one little movement, but I raise my hips so he goes deeper than he intended.

"Fuuuck, Hailey," Kobe groans, while I grab the sheets and scrunch up my eyes. The feeling is unlike anything I've ever felt before. My pussy is on fire, my insides are stretched, and he's only an inch or two in.

"Look at me," Kobe commands.

I peel my eyes open and he's on top of me, breathing hard. "Your tight cunt is going to take me, Hailey."

The dirty words make my mouth pop open in shock as a fresh dampness floods my pussy. He pushes further, this time coming up against my virgin barrier.

Our eyes are locked, and we're breathing hard. He pauses for an agonizing moment. Then he thrusts into me.

There's a stinging sensation and I want to shut my eyes, but I keep them locked on Kobe. He's completely still as I feel the pain subside, and my pussy settles around his cock.

His head dips to mine so our foreheads are touching.

"Are you okay, Beauty?" he whispers.

"Yeah." I nod. I'm better than okay. I've never felt so connected, so full, so happy as I do right now with this man inside of me.

His lips meet mine, and we kiss long and slow as he moves inside of me. And I move with him, creating our own rhythm. Slow at first as I get used to his girth, then faster as our bodies get used to each other. My hips push upward and he slides in even more, making me cry out. I didn't know he could go any further.

Kobe watches his cock sliding in and out of me. Seeing the joy, the desire on his face makes me even more turned on.

His thumb slides to my clit, making small circles as he fucks me. And that's my undoing.

"Kobe," I cry his name as I fall over the edge.

My pussy squeezes his cock, and I don't know how he doesn't explode, but he doesn't.

He stays still, waiting till I stop shaking.

"Wow."

I'm floating. I can barely talk. Kobe's moving my body, and he could do anything to me right now. I'm limp and pliable and all his.

He turns me over so my head is facing the pillow. I get onto my knees and grab the headboard as he lines his cock up with my still pulsing pussy entrance.

"This may feel a little rough."

He's not wrong. I thought I was taking all of him before, but it's nothing compared to what I feel as he sinks deep inside me.

He holds my hips, keeping me in place as he plows into me again and again. My knuckles turn white where I'm gripping the headboard so tight.

"Kobe." I scream his name with every thrust. My pussy is on fire, and I've never felt so full.

One hand grabs my tits and his thumb strums my nipple, and even through his excitement, he's still taking care of me.

"Touch yourself, Hailey."

It's a command, and I do as he says. With my hand between my legs, I feel his slick cock sliding in and out of me as I rub my clit.

"Kobe." I pant his name over and over as the pressure builds inside me.

"Come for me, Hailey. Come for me."

His fingers pinch my nipples, and it's all too much.

I scream as my body thrashes, the orgasm hurtling through my body like a freight train. At the same time, Kobe explodes into me with a roar. Hot come coats my insides as he releases into me.

I bear down on him, my pussy squeezing him for everything he's got until we're both panting and still.

But he's not done with me yet. Kobe flips me over, and I'm still panting as he lowers his face to my pussy and laps up all my juices and the cum that's trickling out of my entrance.

It's so dirty and I love it. My legs stick straight up into the air as I writhe on the bed moaning, feeling like a dirty slut who can't get enough.

Kobe coaxes another orgasm out of me, my pussy shuddering on his face.

Then he's moving up the bed, kissing my breasts and my neck and my mouth. And he's saved some of his cum for me. Oh my god, he pushes his cum into my mouth, and I take it like a good girl. It's warm and thick and hot and I taste my own tangy juices, lapping it all up eagerly.

As his cum dribbles down my chin we kiss hard, sharing each other's juices, our bodies sticky and messy with them.

Kobe's hard again and I roll on top of him, keeping our bodies close and our lips locked as I slide down his beautiful cock. He grabs my hips, pulling me down his shaft at a furious pace. I ride him hard, my body writhing against his as the pressure builds and builds.

Then I'm screaming his name as we both fall over the edge.

I'm flying. My spirit has left my body and it soars above us, looking down at the two of us on the bed together, naked and intertwined.

I hang in the air for a moment. Then I slowly, slowly come down to earth.

We fall onto the bed, exhausted, and Kobe pulls me into his arms. It's not long before his breathing deepens, and I'm about to doze off myself when something tugs at the edge of my consciousness. We didn't use protection.

I sit up in bed, but Kobe doesn't stir.

It felt so good, and in the moment, I didn't even think about protection. I fled my hometown because I didn't want to end up pregnant and tied to a man, but what do I go and do? Let myself get carried away and have unprotected sex with a stranger.

*But he's not a stranger.*

I tell myself to shut up as I climb out of bed. I've been stupid and careless and almost got caught. It's time to move on.

9

KOBE

Soft hands run over my belly, and Hailey's body presses against my back.

"I love you," she murmurs into my ear.

Kisses trail down the back of my neck, the smacking of her lips filling my ears. The kisses turn to bites, nipping at my body. But they're not kisses anymore. They're bullets.

I'm in Iraq and we're under fire, bullets whizzing in the air around me. Pain pierces my leg and it collapses under me. I fall hard to the ground as the bullet shatters my kneecap. There's smoke and dust in the air, turning my unit into shadowy outlines, their shouts lost in the dust cloud.

Rapid fire gunshots come from my left, and a man screams. Then a body is falling toward me, blocking out the light, falling, falling…

I wake with a start, my heart racing. But I'm not in Iraq. I'm in my cabin on Wild Heart Mountain, safe with Hailey in the bed next to me.

It haunts me sometimes. That day four years ago when I was shot and we lost Paul. I roll over, wanting to touch Hailey, to touch something real. But her side of the bed is cold.

That's when I see her standing by the door. She's fully dressed, and she's holding her duffel bag in both hands.

The hammering in my heart increases. Something's wrong. Something's very wrong.

"Hailey?" My voice sounds croaky, and I hate how much I need this woman already. How she's become my everything.

"Can you drive me to the bus station, please?"

I stare at her, not understanding the words. Why would she want the bus station when she belongs here with me?

"The bus station," I repeat like a fucking idiot.

"There's a bus leaving this afternoon that I'd like to catch."

I'm gaping at her as the words penetrate my brain. She's staring out the window, not even able to look at me.

Her words finally sink in. She's catching a bus out of town. Hailey's leaving. The last twenty-four hours meant nothing to her.

But of course she's leaving.

How could a beautiful young woman like Hailey want a ruin of a man like me? I've got scars, I limp, and I'm seventeen years older than her. I was deluding myself thinking a woman like Hailey would stick around.

"I'll get dressed." My voice is mechanical. I barely recognize myself.

She exits the room, leaving me feeling empty and more alone than I've ever felt in my life.

I get out of bed and catch my reflection in the window. The jagged scar running down my face that I try to hide under my beard, the wound on my leg where the bullet entered, leaving a sunken kneecap, and the internal scars, the nightmares and the guilt and the feeling that it was all for nothing.

I'm a monster. Of course Hailey couldn't love someone like me.

With a heavy heart, I pull on my clothes and grab my keys.

I can't even look at her as I walk to the door. We don't say a word as she follows me outside to the pickup truck.

I shared one beautiful weekend with Hailey, but I was an idiot to think she'd stick around forever.

## 10

## HAILEY

The drive down the mountain is excruciating. The cold silence that's descended between us freezes my heart. And it's even worse knowing that I'm responsible for putting it there.

It seemed so clear cut when I made the decision to leave. Lying in Kobe's bed realizing we didn't use protection, and I could already be pregnant.

It's exactly what I didn't want, to be young and knocked up. To be just like all the other girls in my hometown. I want more out of life. I want adventure.

*What if Kobe is the adventure?*

Now that I'm in his pickup speeding to a place where we'll have to say goodbye, I wonder if I made the right decision. By the way my heart hurts when I look at him, I'm pretty sure I've fallen for this guy.

Kobe's looking straight ahead at the road, his jaw set in a grim line. He can't even look at me.

I know it was an abrupt way to end it, but if I stayed any longer, I'd never want to leave. And I'm sure it was only a one night thing for him. I can't be anything special to a brave, gentle man like Kobe.

*But we have a connection.*

The way he looked at me made me feel special, but he's never said anything to make me think it's more than a hook up.

I need to get to the next town and get the morning after pill and forget all about Kobe.

Tears spring into my eyes, and I look out the window. I can't let him see me crying. I brought this on myself.

*What if I'm wrong?*

I've said I'm leaving now. I can't go back, even as I long to throw my arms around him.

We pull up at the bus station, and there still hasn't been a word said between us.

I should feel happy. I should feel lighter. I should feel excited about moving on to my new adventure. But suddenly I have the feeling that I've made a mistake. That I want to go back up the mountain to Kobe's cabin and never ever leave.

"Kobe…" My voice wobbles, but he doesn't even look at me.

"That's your bus." He indicates a Greyhound that's just pulled in. "I'll get your bag." He pulls open his door, and he's gone.

His coldness tears at my heart. But what was I expecting?

I climb out of the pickup and take my bag off him.

I can't look him in the eye. I can't speak. I think I've just made the biggest mistake of my life, but I don't know how to rectify it.

Kobe hands over the bag and gets back in his pickup. He doesn't even say goodbye. Tears sting my eyes, and I put one heavy foot in front of the other and walk away.

*This is what I want,* I tell myself.

I want to keep travelling, to have an adventure. I don't want to get knocked up on the side of a mountain.

Then why does it hurt so much to walk away?

## 11
## KOBE

Snow starts to fall as I watch Hailey walk away, chilling me on the outside as much as on the inside. She's still got my coat on. I insisted she wear it when she left the cabin or she'll freeze on the damn road.

I was so sure we shared a connection. But I was stupid to think Hailey could love someone like me.

On the other side of the street, Angie scurries past with her kids, hustling them home from school before the snow gets heavier. I'm about to pull out and offer them a lift when Corbin pulls up next to them.

The kids pile in the back of his car, and Angie gets in the front. She throws her head back and laughs, and I wonder what the sullen Corbin could have possibly said to make her laugh like that.

Angie was married to Paul for four years before he was killed. They hooked up after he signed up, so she knew the life she was getting into and the risks that come with marrying into the military. I asked her once if she ever regretted it, loving someone that much, knowing you might lose them.

She thought I was ridiculous.

"He gave me four years of absolute happiness," she said. "You'd be a fool to regret that."

As I watch Hailey walk away, I think about those words. Am I a being a fool, letting her slip away like this without even telling her how I feel?

If I'm honest with myself, I'm terrified. If I tell her how I feel and she rejects me, it'll confirm everything I know: that I'm not worthy of a woman like Hailey. But if I never tell her, how will I ever know if I missed my chance for happiness?

Seizing the door with determination, I throw it open and stride toward the line of people waiting for the bus. My hands are sweaty despite the cold, and my pulse is racing.

Going to war was a terrifying experience, but I don't think I've ever been as scared as when I stride over to Hailey.

The woman holds my heart in her hands. My future happiness depends on what happens in the next few minutes. She will either crush me or make me whole.

"Hailey."

My hand thumps down on her shoulder, and she jumps. I've startled her, again proving what an oaf I am. I almost back away, but when she turns around her eyes are red from crying. When she sees me they widen, a hopeful expression coming over her face.

I talk quickly before I can chicken out.

"Hailey, we've only known each other for a few days. Less than a few days, about twenty-four hours, or maybe a bit less…"

I'm bumbling, and it's not coming out right. I look around in frustration, but there's no unit here to back me up. I'm all on my own in the trenches.

I take a deep breath and start again.

"I knew the moment I saw you that you were someone special. You make me forget the bad things and remember the good things, like joy and hope. You make me feel alive in a way that I haven't felt since I came back from Iraq…"

Man, this is hard. She's looking at me intently, letting me talk, and I still have no idea if my feelings are reciprocated.

"I know I'm old. I know I'm broken. I know I'm scarred. And I know I'm not the adventure you're looking for. But is there any chance you could ever love a man like me?"

I've never felt so vulnerable. I've never felt so afraid. I've never felt how precious my heart is, that someone can hold it in their hands and have the absolute power to crush me or lift me up.

"Kobe." She fists the lapels of my jacket. "I already love you."

She pulls on the lapels of my jacket for emphasis.

"Then why are you leaving?" The relief is immense, but I'm still confused.

"I left my hometown because I didn't want to settle down and have babies like everybody else. But since I've met you, all I want to do is settle down and have babies. And that terrifies me."

Her words make my soul sing. She loves me. Sleeping Beauty loves me.

"Oh, honey. Is that what you're worried about?"

She nods. "I felt so comfortable in your arms, in your cabin, and I freaked out about letting myself down. I'm not having the adventure that I should have. But I was wrong, Kobe, I don't want to leave. I want to stay with you on the mountain."

I clasp her hands in mine, and they're freezing cold. I press them to my lips, trying to breathe warmth back into them. I've got to get this woman some damn winter clothes.

"Hailey, I promise you that if you stay with me, I'll make the rest of your life an adventure.

"I love you, Hailey. I want you next to me on my mountain. If you don't want babies straight away, that's fine. If you don't want babies at all, that's fine. I just want you."

Tears spring to her eyes, and from the way she's grinning at me, I guess they're happy tears.

"Kobe, that's the thing. You make me want to have babies. It's the most irritating thing in the world."

I throw my head back and laugh, and it's an alien sound. But with this woman I feel parts of me waking up that have been asleep for too long.

Snow flurries around her golden locks and land on her exposed head because she's not wearing a goddamn hat either.

"Tomorrow we're going shopping," I say as I pull her to the truck.

"What for?"

"For some goddamn winter clothes. If you're gonna spend winter here you need more than a wooly sweater."

She leans into me, and I put my arm around her.

"That's what I've got you for. To keep me warm."

As she says it her hand travels over my chest, sending a shock of heat through my body and making my cock instantly hard.

The snow's falling harder now, and I fling her bag in the back and open the passenger door.

She scoots over, and I climb in my side and meet

her halfway. Now that I know she loves me, I can't keep my hands off her.

We kiss in the front cab of the truck like horny teenagers. But once I get started, I can't stop.

Her desire is as urgent as mine, and we devour each other with our lips.

Hailey climbs onto my lap, undoing my belt buckle as she straddles me.

I peek out the window, but the bus is gone and the town is empty, everyone driven inside by the snow.

But I don't care if anyone sees us. I want the world to know that this woman is mine.

We awkwardly pull at each other's clothing until I've got her leggings around her ankles and my cock is popped out of my pants.

I'd prefer her fully naked, but there's something sexy about this quickie in the front seat.

She's slick and wet, and this time I don't need to warm her up. She slides down my cock, and I love that she's taking control. Her eyes widen as my girth fills her up. My cock slides into her tight cunt, making me groan at how good it feels.

I thrust my hips, making me go deeper, and she squeezes her eyes shut.

"Eyes on me, baby." She flicks them open. "I want to watch you as I make love to my future wife."

Her eyes go even wider, and I use the opportunity to grab her hips and thrust deeper.

She cries out as I impale her on the end of my cock, and it feels so good to be inside her knowing that she's mine. Hailey is all mine.

Her hands grab my shoulder as she rides my cock. We're restricted by the space in the cab, but it just makes it more intense. Her thighs grind into my side, and her clit rubs against me.

"Kobe," she pants into my ear. "I'm gonna come soon."

"Good girl. Come like a good girl."

The windows have steamed up and the pickup's rocking, and anybody who saw us would know exactly what we're doing in here. But I don't give a fuck. Let everyone know Hailey is mine. I claim her. She's my mountain woman. I'm taking her back to my cabin to be mine forever.

"Kobe, Kobe. Oh Kobe..." she pants. And the way she says my name makes my balls pull up tight. I'm ready for her, and as soon as she cries out and I feel her pussy contract I let myself go, exploding deep inside of her, coating her womb with my seed.

Her nails dig into my shoulder as her body rocks.

I'll have marks tomorrow where she's clung onto me, but these are scars I'll happily wear.

Hailey makes me feel alive. I know that without

this woman I would still be a broken man. She's made me whole, and for that I'll be forever thankful.

# EPILOGUE

## HAILEY

Eight years later…

"Look at all the tomatoes I picked." Noah hands me a bowl of tomatoes with a proud smile on his three-year-old face.

It's a mixture of red and green and orange cherry tomatoes and only about half of them are ripe enough to go into the salad, but I don't tell him that.

"Thank you, sweetie. You're so helpful."

He beams at me. "Do you need lettuce, mommy?"

"Sure."

Noah toddles out the back door with a new purpose, heading to the vegetable patch I cultivated in the back yard.

It's hard to grow vegetables in this mountain climate, but we have a good greenhouse and I tend to them most days. Most of the ingredients going into the salad tonight will be from our own garden.

We've got Dylon and Rhys coming over for dinner tonight with their wives and kids.

I swear if we didn't organize anything they would be total recluses, but Kobe makes an effort with his former Marine buddies. He still meets the guys every month at Angie's bar, and we take turns hosting dinners, sometimes with all of the families getting together at once.

When I set off from my hometown eight years ago, I went looking for adventure. And I found it here on the mountain.

In the eight years since I've been here, I've not once regretted my decision to stay.

I thought that I didn't want to settle down with kids and be a housewife, but I love the domestic life. Being with Kobe is the biggest adventure of my life. Every day is different, and every day I'm grateful for him and our kids.

I watch him out the window helping the kids pick lettuce leaves. He's cradling the baby in one arm as he crouches next to Noah. Our oldest, Rolf, at five years old, is bringing in the wood for the fire tonight. He's a big boy already, like his daddy, and learning how to be a mountain man just like him.

A wave of gratitude ripples through me so strongly that I grip the sides of the kitchen counter. I can't believe how good my life is, and I can't believe I almost missed out on all this.

Kobe must feel my eyes on him, because he turns around and our gazes lock through the glass. He gives me one of his wide smiles that are common on his rugged face these days. My husband still walks with a limp and he still has his scars, but his family has given him a new life, a new purpose.

His gaze lingers on me, and just from one look my nipples go hard. For the first time, I regret that we've got friends coming over tonight. But I know once they've gone home, me and Kobe will share some time together.

The phone rings, and I dry my hands on a dish-cloth as I grab it from my back pocket. It's Trish giving me an update on what's happening at the shelter today.

Yeah, I found my purpose in life, being a wife and mother and helping women in need. I finally convinced Trish to leave that douchebag and move to the mountain. Together, we founded a refuge up here in the mountains for women needing a safe place. But how all that came about is a story for another time…

## TAKEN BY THE MOUNTAIN MAN

**She's alone in the woods, mine to take, mine to protect...**

When I discover the frightened woman camping on her own with a storm coming, my protective instincts kick in.

There's an evacuee center in town, but there's no way I'm taking Leonie anywhere but my mountain cabin.

Something's got her spooked, and I'll stand guard all night if that's what makes her feel safe.

But when the new day dawns, there's no way I'm giving Leonie up.

This curvy beauty is mine.

*Taken by the Mountain Man* is a forced proximity, age gap, instalove romance featuring an ex-military mountain man and the curvy, innocent woman he takes as his own.

Read Taken By the Mountain Man next.

* * *

Also mentioned in this book…

Hailey's sister Trish is a single mom in danger. Can she find happiness with an ex-military recluse?
Read Trish's story in Wild Runaway.

# GET YOUR FREE BOOKS

Sign up to the Sadie King mailing list and get access to all the bonus content including bonus scenes and five FREE steamy short romances!

You'll be the first to hear about new releases, exclusive offers, bonus content and all my news. You can even email me back. I love chatting with my readers!

To claim your free books visit:
authorsadieking.com/bonus-scenes

If you're already a subscriber check your last email for the link that will take you straight to the bonus content.

# ABOUT THE AUTHOR

Sadie King is a USA Today Best Selling Author of over 120 short and steamy contemporary romances. She loves writing about military heroes and the sassy women who heal their hearts.

Sadie lives in New Zealand with her ex-military husband and raucous young son.

When she's not writing she loves catching waves with her son, running along the beach, and drinking good wine, preferably with a book in hand.

Sign up to her newsletter to receive all the latest news and releases and access to exclusive bonus content.

www.authorsadieking.com

# THANK YOU

Thank you for reading my story! If you enjoyed it, please consider leaving a review, they mean so much to authors and it helps other readers find books they might enjoy.

Thank you!
Sadie xx